The World's Greatest Singer

by Lily Wagner
illustrated by Celine Malepart

Harcourt
SCHOOL PUBLISHERS

Printed in China

ISBN 10: 0-15-350525-7
ISBN 13: 978-0-15-350525-6

Ordering Options
ISBN 10: 0-15-350334-3 (Grade 4 Below-Level Collection)
ISBN 13: 978-0-15-350334-4 (Grade 4 Below-Level Collection)
ISBN 10: 0-15-357517-4 (package of 5)
ISBN 13: 978-0-15-357517-4 (package of 5)

2 3 4 5 6 7 8 9 10 985 12 11 10 09 08 07

Abby squeezed into the back of the car. Her mother, two brothers, and her sister were waiting for her.

"You're a little late. Is everything all right, Abby?" asked Mom.

"Ms. Robinson just wanted to ask me about something," said Abby. "She asked me to try out for the school play, but I said no."

"She probably was actually asking Abby *not* to sing in the school play," Allison said. Adam and Alan slapped high-fives with Allison as Abby glared at them.

Mom turned around and said, “That’s enough, everybody. Abby can sing just as well as anyone.”

Adam, Alan, and Allison looked at each other and cracked up again. Abby just stared out the window.

“Abby, don’t listen to them,” said Mom. “You could sing if you tried. Why not just try out for the play?”

“Why bother? I can’t sing as well as they do, or you, or Dad,” Abby said in a despairing voice.

It was true, whether anyone wanted to admit it or not. Everyone in the family except for Abby had great voices. They had the kind of voices that made people want to stop and listen. They all were in singing groups and performed in community theater. Allison and Adam had sung backup vocals on a famous recording artist's song. Meanwhile, Abby had a plain, slightly scratchy voice. She couldn't sing very high, but she also couldn't sing very low.

That night, Mom came to talk to Abby. "Not everyone has to sing, you know," she said. "You paint beautiful pictures, you're a wonderful swimmer, and you're so imaginative and resourceful."

Mom gave Abby a big hug, turned off the lights, and left. Abby knew Mom's intentions were good, but she had inadvertently made Abby feel worse. She wanted to be like her family. She felt left out when they sang together.

"I wish I were the world's greatest singer," thought Abby as she drifted off to sleep.

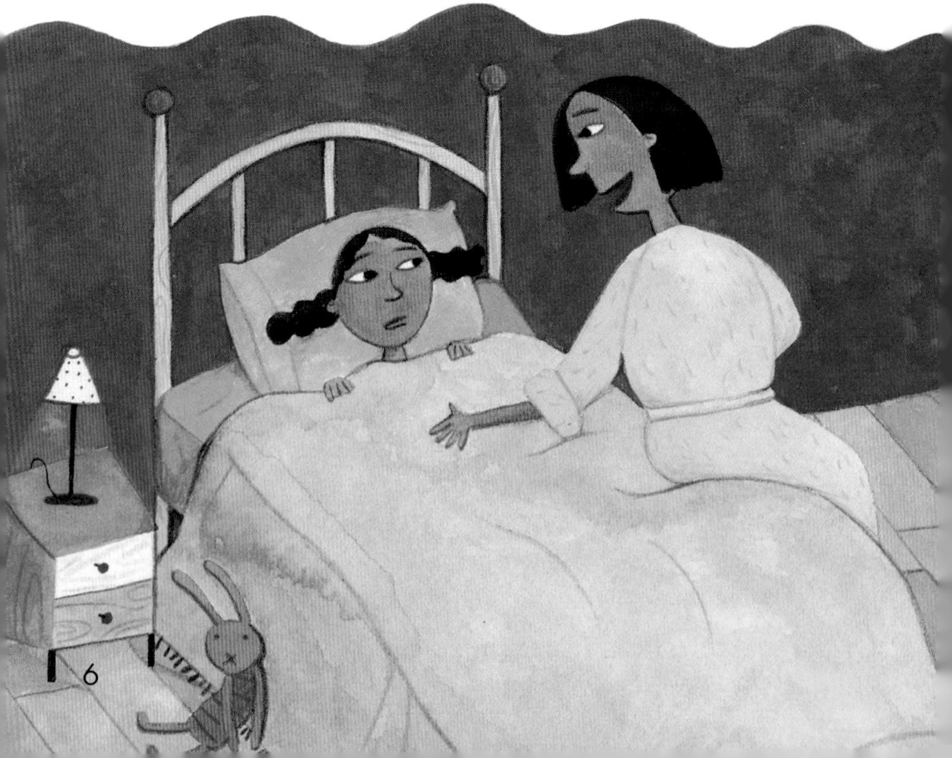

Abby was roused by the relentless sound of a cell phone ringing. She was about to go back to sleep when she heard her mother's voice. Mom was sitting by her bed, talking on the phone about something to do with a show.

Mom flipped the phone shut and said, "All right, Abby, time to go."

"Go where?" Abby mumbled sleepily.

"You're doing the *Hello Morning* show, and then we're going to Felicia's office to pick out some clothes for the photo shoot this afternoon," said Mom briskly.

Mom turned on the light, and Abby realized that they were in a hotel room. Before she could ask any questions, Mom hurried Abby into clothes she didn't recognize, and then they went out the door to a waiting car.

When the car stopped, security guards escorted them past a screaming crowd into a building. Abby was whisked into a room with mirrors and lights, where people put makeup on her. After that, they were led into a waiting room. There was a table with a bountiful display of food, but Abby wasn't hungry.

"Mom, what's going on?" Abby whispered.

Mom scanned a schedule. "You're on next, and you're singing 'Sunshine.'"

Abby's heart plummeted to her feet. Sing? There must be a mistake. She didn't have a chance to ask, though. A man rushed in and told them to follow him. Before she could say anything, Abby was on an outdoor stage in front of a microphone. Suddenly, she looked out into the vast crowd and saw a sign that said, "Abby Bowen, World's Greatest Singer!"

Music began to play, and without even thinking, Abby began to sing. It was a voice she'd never heard before. It sounded rich and confident and thrilling. When she finished, the crowd burst into applause. Abby stood there a moment, and then she understood that her wish had been granted!

The crowd was waiting when Abby left the building. They begged her for autographs and asked her to pose for photographs. Abby wrote her name and smiled for the pictures.

"I can't believe this is happening to me!" she thought happily.

Afterward, Abby and her mom went to a magazine editor's office where Abby posed for more photographs. At first, it felt strange, but then it started to be fun.

Next they went to a studio where a voice teacher went over a new song with Abby. Abby was worried about singing—what if she couldn't do it again? However, the beautiful voice was still there. For the first time ever, Abby enjoyed singing. She couldn't believe how quickly the afternoon passed.

Abby easily got used to her new stature as a star. Her days were filled with rehearsals, photo shoots, and interviews. She and Mom traveled to many exciting cities. When she called home, Allison, Alan, and Adam complimented her singing.

"Now who's the best singer in the family?" Abby thought smugly.

Of course, she didn't have much time to talk to her friends. Sometimes she read Mallory's e-mails about swim team or Taylor's stories about a big party. Then one day, she had a strange thought: "I wish I were with them."

It seemed impossible that she would feel that way. She was talented, she was famous, and her life was endlessly exciting. However, Abby realized that she missed her old life.

One day, Abby said she was sick. They cancelled shows and took her to a doctor. He told her to rest and that she would be fine. Then everything picked up again. She tried singing badly. Her voice still sounded perfect, though, no matter how hard she tried to sing off key. She couldn't stop being the World's Greatest Singer.

"I wish I were my real self again," she thought. "I wish I were the world's worst singer!"

When Abby woke up the next morning, she was back in her own room! Everything was exactly the same as when she had last seen it.

"It was a dream!" thought Abby. She just needed to test something. Abby sang at the top of her lungs. She sounded awful!

Adam looked into her room and shook his head. "I hate to say it, Abby, but you've got to be the world's worst singer."

Abby smiled joyfully. "Thank you!"

Think Critically

1. What is the moral, or lesson, of this story?

2. Why do you think Abby's teacher wanted her to be in the play?

3. What part of this story could be real? What part is fantasy?

4. Do you think Abby is really the world's worst singer? Explain your answer.

5. Would you choose to go back to your ordinary life like Abby did? Why or why not?

Language Arts

Change the Ending Think about another way the story could have ended. Then write your new ending.

School-Home Connection Share this story with a family member. Then talk about funny or interesting dreams you have had.

Word Count: 1,042